T0197518

The

Art Easels

that Came

to Life

B.I PHILLIPS

To order additional copies of this book, contact:
Xlibris
844-714-8691
www.Xlibris.com
Orders@Xlibris.com

ISBN: Softcover   978-1-6641-9687-2
         EBook   978-1-6641-9688-9

Print information available on the last page

Rev. date: 11/05/2021

This book belongs to:

_____

ACKNOWLEDGEMENT

GRATEFUL ACKNOWLEDGEMENTS
TO YMCA AND GAINOR ROBERTS

The ladies are taking an art class in which they are all painting dogs.

Suddenly, the art easels spring to life and the dogs jump out of the paintings. The canvasses fall to the floor.

The dogs go and make cookies.

The Art easels go to yoga.

The Art easels go fishing.

The Art easels go to beach.

Island vacation.

Single family Christmas.

It was about opposites.

The art easels get tired of having no life and holding the paintings so they come to life and then start having fun.

Then the people - artists start holding the paintings so the easels can paint.

It's magical. Of course.

Printed in the United States
by Baker & Taylor Publisher Services